Dream Weaver

BY JANE YOLEN

Illustrated by Michael Hague

PHILOMEL BOOKS   NEW YORK

For David, in all my dreams

Published by Philomel books, a division of The Putnam & Grosset Group,
200 Madison Avenue, New York, NY 10016. Published simultaneously in Canada.
All rights reserved. Original edition published in 1979 by
William Collins Publishers, Inc., Cleveland and New York. "Brother Hart,"
"The Tree's Wife" and "The Pot Child," copyright © 1978 By Jane Yolen,
first appeared in The Magazine of Fantasy and Science Fiction.
"Princess Heart O'Stone" and "The Cat Bride"
first appeared in Cricket Magazine.
Text copyright © 1979 and 1989 by Jane Yolen
Illustrations copyright © 1979 and 1989 by Michael Hague
Printed in The United States of America.

Library of Congress Cataloging in Publication Data
Yolen, Jane H. Dream Weaver
Summary: For a penny a dream, the old blind Dream Weaver weaves dreams
for seven sets of passers-by. 1. Fairy tales, American. {1. Fairy tales}
I. Hague, Michael.   II. Title PZ8.Y78Dr {Fic} 78-26982
ISBN 0-399-22152-2
First revised edition

CONTENTS

INTRODUCTION

The stories that touch us—child and adult—most deeply are, like our myths, crafted visions, shaped dreams. They are not the smaller dreams that you and I have each night, rehearsals of things to come or anticipation/dread turned into impenetrable symbols, but the larger dreams that belong to all humankind, or as the Dream Weaver says, "The heart and soul made visible."

The stories in this book—like all stories—were not created out of pure neverneverland. They are resonances of the teller's life: my life. They are part of memory, that "Daughter of the ear and eye" as the Dream Weaver tells her audience.

For example "The Boy Who Sang for Death" had much to do with my mourning my own beloved mother, dead at age fifty-nine of lung cancer. "The Pot Child" was, in part, fashioned after a potter friend who worked in our barn and in part an answer to a particular critic who had been very harsh and negative about my work. "Brother Hart" came from my childhood love of the Grimm story Number 11, "Brother and Sister."

When I wrote the stories for *Dream Weaver*, a national renaissance in the art of storytelling was just beginning. Tellers were plucking tales out of books, out of the mouths of family members, out of their own hearts. Some of them told stories in schools and libraries, some in churches and synagogues, some in hospitals and hospices, some in coffee houses and on the stage, and some—as my Dream Weaver does—to passers-by in the streets.

Today many of the tales I invented for this book are being told by those same tellers. I heard a rendition of "The Pot Child" at a library conference. I heard "The Tree's Wife" told at a women's seminar. And I listened with pleasure to a teller bring "The Cat Bride" to life on the stage of a large theater. I love knowing that these stories I labored so hard over have a life of their own off the pages. It means I have touched people and the magic has been passed on. And on.

We are what we tell: my story, your story, our story—
HISTORY.

—Jane Yolen
HATFIELD,
MASSACHUSETTS, 1989

Dream Weaver

"*A* penny, a penny, kind sir," cried the Dream Weaver as she sat at the bottom steps of the Great Temple. Her busy fingers worked the small hand loom. "Just a penny for a woven dream."

The King of Beggars passed her by. He had no time for dream weaving. It was too gossamer, too fragile. He believed in only one dream, that which would fill his belly. He would not part with his penny for any other. Gathering his rags around him, a movement he considered his answer, he went on.

The Old Dream Weaver continued her wail. It was a chant, an obeisance she made to every passer-by. She did not see the King of Beggar's gesture for she was blind. Her sightless eyes stared only into the future, and she wove by the feel of the strands.

New footsteps came to the Dream Weaver's ear. Her hand went out.

"A penny, a penny, young miss." She knew by the sound there was a girl approaching, for the step was light and dancing.

"Oh, yes, buy me a dream," the girl said, calling over her shoulder to the boy who followed.

The Weaver did not speak again. She knew better than to wheedle. The girl was already caught in her desire. The young so loved to dream. The Weaver knew the penny would come.

"I do not know if I should," said the boy. His voice was hesitant, yet pleased to be asked.

"Of course you should," said the girl. Then her voice dropped, and she moved close to him. "Please."

His hand went immediately to his pocket and drew out the coin. Hearing the movement, the Dream Weaver cupped her right

9

hand. "*A dream for a beautiful young woman,*" *she said in a flattering voice, though to her all the young were beautiful.*

"*How do you know?*" *It was the girl in surprise.*

"*She* is *beautiful,*" *said the boy. "There is no one as beautiful in the whole world. She has my heart.*" *His words were genuine, but the girl shrugged away his assurances.*

The Weaver had already taken threads from her basket and strung the warp while the boy was speaking. And this was the dream that she wove across the strands.

❧ Brother Hart ❧

Deep in a wood, so dark and tangled few men dared enter it, there was a small clearing. And in that clearing lived a girl and her brother Hart.

By day, in his deer shape, Brother Hart would go out and forage on green grass and budlings while his sister remained at home.

But whenever dusk began, the girl Hinda would go to the edge of the clearing and call out in a high, sweet voice:

> Dear heart, Brother Hart,
> Come at my behest.
> We shall dine on berry wine
> And you shall have your rest.

Then, in his deer heart, her brother would know the day's enchantment was at an end and run swiftly home. There, at the lintel over the cottage door, he would rub between his antlers until the hide on his forehead broke bloodlessly apart.

He would rub and rub further still until the brown hide skinned back along both sides and he stepped out a naked man.

His sister would take the hide and shake it out and brush and comb it until it shone like polished wood. Then she hung the hide up by the antlers beside the door, with the legs dangling down. It would hang there until the morning when Brother Hart donned it once again and raced off to the lowland meadows to graze.

What spell or sorcerer had brought them there, deep in the wood, neither could recall. Their faces mirrored one another, and their lives were twinned. Their memories, like the sorcerer, had vanished. The woods, the meadow, the clearing, the deer hide, the cottage door, were all they knew.

Now one day in late spring, Brother Hart had gone as usual to the lowland meadows, leaving Hinda at home. She had washed and scrubbed the little cottage until it was neat and clean. She had put new straw in their bedding. But as she stood by the window brushing out her long dark hair, an unfamiliar sound greeted her ears: a loud, harsh calling, neither bird nor jackal nor good grey wolf.

Again and again the call came. So Hinda went to the door, for she feared nothing in the wood. And who should come winded to the cottage but Brother Hart. He had no words to tell her in his deer form, but blood beaded his head like a crown. It was the first time she had ever seen him bleed. He pushed past her and collapsed, shivering, on their bed.

Hinda ran over to him and would have bathed him with her tears, but the jangling noise called out again, close and insistent. She ran to the window to see.

There was a man outside in the clearing. At least she thought it was a man. Yet he did not look like Brother Hart, who was the only man she knew.

He was large where Brother Hart was slim. He was fair where Brother Hart was dark. He was hairy where Brother Hart was smooth. And he was dressed in animal skins that hung from his shoulders to his feet. About the man leaped fawning wolves, some spotted like jackals, some tan and some white. He pushed them from him with a rough sweep of his hand.

"I seek a deer," he called when he glimpsed Hinda's face, a pale moon, at the window.

But when Hinda came out of the door, closing it behind her to hide what lay inside, the man did not speak again. Instead he took off his fur hat and laid it upon his heart, kneeling down before her.

"Who are you?" asked Hinda. "What are you? And why do you seek the deer?" Her voice was gentle but firm.

The man neither spoke nor rose but stared at her face.

"Who are you?" Hinda asked again. "Say what it is you are."

As if she had broken a spell, the man spoke at last. "I am but a man," he said. "A man who has traveled far and who has seen much, but never a beauty such as yours."

"If it *is* beauty, and beauty is what you prize, you shall not see it again," said Hinda. "For a man who hunts the deer can be no friend of mine."

The man rose then, and Hinda marveled at the height of him, for he was as tall as the cottage door and his hands were grained like wood.

"Then I shall hunt the deer no more," he said, "if you will give me leave to hunt that which is now all at once dearer to me."

"And what is that?"

"You, dear heart," he said, reaching for her. Startled, Hinda moved away from him but, remembering her brother inside the cottage, found voice to say, "Tomorrow." She reached behind her and steadied herself on the door handle. She thought she heard the heavy breathing of Brother Hart through the walls. "Come tomorrow."

"I shall surely come." He bowed, turned, and then was gone, walking swiftly, a man's stride, through the woods. His animals were at his heels.

Hinda's eyes followed him down the path until she counted even the shadows of trees as his own. When she was certain he was gone, she opened the cottage door and went in. The cottage was suddenly close and dark, filled with the musk of deer.

Brother Hart lay on their straw bed. When he looked up at her, Hinda could not bear the twin wounds of his eyes. She turned away and said, "You may go out now. It is safe. He will not hunt you again."

The deer rose heavily to his feet, nuzzled open the door, and sprang away to the meadows.

But he was home again at dark.

When he stepped out of his skin and entered the cottage, he did not greet his sister with his usual embrace. Instead he said, "You did not call me to the clearing. You did not say my name. Only when I was tired and the sun had almost gone, did I know it was time to come home."

Hinda could not answer. She could not even look at him. For even more than his words, his nakedness suddenly shamed her. She put their food on the table and they ate their meal in silence. Then they lay down together and slept without dreams like the wild creatures of the wood.

When the sun called Brother Hart to his deerskin once again, Hinda opened the door. Silently she ushered him outside, silently watched him change, and sent him off on his silent way to the meadows without word of farewell. Her thoughts were on the hunter, the man of the wolves. She never doubted he would come.

And come he did, neither silently nor slowly, but with loud purposeful steps. He stood for a moment at the clearing's edge, looking at Hinda, measuring her with his eyes. Then he smiled and crossed to her.

He stayed all the day with her and taught her wonders she had never known. He told her tales of kingdoms she had never seen. He sang songs she had never heard before, singing them softly into her ears. He spoke again and again of his love for her, but he touched no more than her hand.

"You are as innocent as any creature in the woods," he said over and over in amazement.

So passed the day.

Suddenly it was dusk, and Hinda looked up with a start. "You must go now," she said.

"Nay, I must stay."

"No no, you must go," Hinda said again. "I cannot have you here at night. If you love me, go." Then she added softly, her dark eyes on his, "But come again in the morning."

Her sudden fear puzzled him, but it also touched him, so

14

he stood and smoothed down the skins of his coat. "I will go. But I will return."

He whistled his animals to him, and left the clearing as swiftly as he had come.

Hinda would have called after him then, called after and made him stay, but she did not even know his name. So she went instead to the clearing's edge and cried:

Dear Heart, Brother Hart,
Come at my bidding.
We shall dine on berry wine
And dance at my wedding.

And hearing her voice, Brother Hart raced home.

He stopped at the clearing's edge, raised his head, and sniffed. The smell of man hung on the air, heavy and threatening. He came through it as if through a swift current, and stepped to the cottage door.

Rubbing his head more savagely than ever on the lintel, as if to rip off his thoughts with his hide, Brother Hart removed his skin.

"The hunter was here," he said as he crossed the threshold of the door.

"He does not seek you," Hinda replied.

"You will not see him again. You will tell him to go."

"I see him for your sake," said Hinda. "If he sees me, he does not see you. If he hunts me, he does not hunt you. I do it for you, brother dear."

Satisfied, Brother Hart sat down to eat. But Hinda was not hungry. She served her brother and watched as he ate his fill.

"You should sleep," she said when he was done. "Sleep, and I will rub your head and sing to you."

"I *am* tired," he answered. "My head aches where yesterday he struck me. My heart aches still with the fear. I tremble all over. You are right. I should sleep."

So he lay down on the bed and Hinda sat by him. She rubbed cinquefoil on his head to soothe it and sang him many songs, and soon Brother Hart was asleep.

When the moon lit the clearing, the hunter returned. He could not wait until the morning. Hinda's fear had made him afraid, though he had never known fear before. He dared not leave her alone in the forest. But he moved quietly as a beast in the dark. He left his dogs behind.

The cottage in the clearing was still except for a breath of song, wordless and longing, that floated on the air. It was Hinda's voice, and when the hunter heard it, he smiled for she was singing a tune he had taught her.

He moved out into the clearing, more boldly now. Then suddenly he stopped. He saw a strange shape hanging by the cottage door. It was a deerskin, a fine buck's hide, hung by the antlers and the legs dangling down.

Caution, an old habit, claimed him. He circled the clearing, never once making a sound. He approached the cottage from the side, and Hinda's singing led him on. When he reached the window, he peered in.

Hinda was sitting on a low straw bed, and beside her, his head in her lap, lay a man. The man was slim and naked and dark. His hair was long and straight and came to his shoulders. The hunter could not see his face, but he lay in sleep like a man who was no stranger to the bed.

16

The hunter controlled the shaking of his hands, but he could not control his heart. He allowed himself one moment of fierce anger. With his knife he thrust a long gash on the left side of the deerskin that hung by the door. Then he was gone.

In the cottage Brother Hart cried out in his sleep, a swift sharp cry. His hand went to his side and suddenly, under his heart, a thin red line like a knife's slash appeared. It bled for a moment. Hinda caught his hand up in hers and at the sight of the blood she grew pale. It was the second time she had seen Brother Hart bleed.

She got up without disturbing him and went to the cupboard where she found a white linen towel. She washed the wound with water. The cut was long, but it was not deep. Some scratch he had got in the woods perhaps. She knew it would heal before morning. So she lay down beside him and fitted her body to the curve of his back. Brother Hart stirred slightly but did not waken. Then Hinda, too, fell asleep.

In the morning Brother Hart rose, but his movements were slow. "I wish I could stay," he said to his sister. "I wish this enchantment were at an end."

But the rising sun summoned him outside. He donned the deerskin and leaped away.

Hinda stood at the door and raised her hand to shade her eyes. The last she saw of him was the flash of white tail as he sped off into the woods.

She did not go back into the cottage to clean. She stood waiting for the hunter to come. Her eyes and ears strained for the signs of his approach. There were none.

She waited through the whole of the long morning, until the sun was high overhead. Not until then did she go indoors, where she threw herself down on the straw bedding and wept.

At dusk the sun began to fade and the cottage darkened. Hinda got up. She went out to the clearing's edge and called:

Dear heart, Brother Hart,
Come at my crying.
We shall dine on berry wine
And . . .

But she got no further. A loud sound in the woods stayed her. It was too heavy for a deer. And when the hunter stepped out of the woods on the very path that Brother Hart usually took, Hinda gave a gasp, part delight, part fear.

"You have come," she said, and her voice trembled.

The hunter searched her face with his eyes but could not find what he was seeking. He walked past her to the cottage door. Hinda followed behind him, uncertain.

"I have come," he said. His back was to her. "I wish to God I had not."

"What do you mean?"

"I sought the deer today," he said.

Hinda's hand went to her mouth.

"I sought the deer today. And what I seek, I find." He did not turn. "We ran him long, my dogs and I. When he was at bay, he fought hard. I gave the beast's liver and heart to my dogs. But this I saved for you."

He held up his hands then, and a deerskin unrolled from it.

18

With a swift, savage movement, he tacked it to the door with his knife. The hooves did not quite touch the ground.

Hinda could see two slashes in the hide, one on each side, under the heart. The slash on the left was an old wound, crusted but clean. The slash on the right was new, and from it blood still dripped.

She leaned forward and touched the wound with her hand, tears in her eyes. "Oh, my dear Brother Hart," she cried. "It was because of me you died. Now your enchantment *is* at an end."

The hunter whirled around to face her then. "He was your brother?" he asked.

She nodded. "He was my heart." Looking straight at him, she added, "We were one at birth. What was his is mine by right." Her chin was up, and her head held high. She reached past the hunter and pulled the knife from the door with an ease that surprised him. Gently she took down the skin. She shook it out once, and smoothed the nap with her hand. Then, as if putting on a cloak, she wrapped the skin around her shoulders and pulled the head over her own.

As the hunter watched, she began to change. It was as if he saw a rippled reflection in a pool coming slowly into focus: slim brown legs, brown haunch, brown body and head. The horns shriveled and fell to the ground. Only her eyes remained the same.

The doe looked at the hunter for a moment more. A single tear started in her eye, but before it had time to fall, she turned, sprang away into the fading light, and was gone.

The dream was finished. The Weaver's hand stopped.

"I would have kept them both," said the girl. "No need to lose one man for another."

"You will never lose me," the boy said quickly, with such yearning in his voice that the Dream Weaver knew he would never have this girl.

"Never," said the girl. "It was a foolish dream. Not even worth the penny."

"I thought it moving," said the boy in a whisper to the Dream Weaver as the girl moved off. "I felt the slash under my heart." His voice broke on the last word. Then he turned and followed the girl.

The Dream Weaver listened to them go, the girl's steps always a bit faster, always anticipating the boy's.

She ripped the skein from the loom and finished it off, putting the fabric in a bag by her side. She sent out a sigh into the air. "People never want to keep their dreams," she said to herself, patting the bag. "I wonder why?"

She heard a carriage come around the corner, the horses blowing gustily through their noses. A heavy carriage by the sound, and rich, for there were four horses. The carriage stopped near the Dream Weaver's place. Her hand went up at once, and her cry began again: "A penny, a penny, a penny for a dream."

An old couple stepped out of the landau. They were richly dressed in the brightest of colors, as if reds and golds could deny their years. Though the woman put her hand on the man's arm to be steadied, there was no warmth for either of them in the touch. And when they talked, as they did for a moment in sharp angry bursts, they did not look into one another's eyes but always stared an inch or two away, concentrating on the collarbone, on a lock of hair, on the lines etched in the forehead.

They would have passed by the Dream Weaver, but the old woman stumbled. The Dream Weaver heard the faulty step and put her raised hand up to help.

In a swift, practiced movement, the man reached into his pocket and paid off the Dream Weaver, as if she were a beggar in the street.

"Please, sir," said the Dream Weaver, for the touch of his hand told her that he was a man; the size of the coin, his peerage. "Please, sir, for the coin, let me weave you a dream."

"We have no time for such mystic nonsense," the man began. Impatiently he looked up at the Great Temple and shook his head.

"It takes but a moment in the weaving, a moment in the telling, but it is beyond time for it will last forever," said the Dream Weaver.

The old man glanced at the sky, judging the time once more, and clicked his tongue. "Forever?" he said, and hesitated.

"A moment," said the Dream Weaver, counting his hesitation as consent. Her fingers scuttled over the warp, and this was the dream that she wove.

❧ Man of Rock, Man of Stone ❧

There was once a quarrier named Craig, who worked stone down in a pit. Stone before him and stone behind, he labored each day from dark to dark. He was a tall man and broad, a mountain working a mountain. The years of his pit work were printed in dust upon his face and grained in the backs of his hands.

He worked alone and spoke not even to himself, except to curse the sun when it shone full upon him or when it did not. And the habit of silence and curses was as engrained in him as the dust.

At home he was like the rocks of his quarry: silent, unmoving, stolid before anyone who would weather him. He was a man of stone.

He had married a woman who was soft where he was hard, and moved by every tenderness he had forgotten. She never gave up trying to water him with her tears as if he were a plant capable of growth. But he was not. He was a man of stone.

Only in the quarry, under the hot eye of the sun, did he take on a semblance of life. There, his hammer above him, he would suck in a breath of dust, then ram the hammer down, expelling dust from his lungs. He took great pride in the sweat that ran down the solid line of his back and stained his clothes, proof of the life within him.

But when the sun went down, life ended for him. He would pack his hammer and chisels into a greyed and cracked satchel and go home.

"Wife," he would call at the door as if he had forgotten her name or thought it too soft for his lips, "I'd eat."

23

His wife had a name, as soft and pliant as the memory of her youth that still hovered about her lips: Cybele. But if she thought of herself at all now, it was as Wife. The rest was gone.

She had been given to the quarrier by her father, one stone gifting another. She was to keep Craig's house, to feed him, and to warm his bed, no more. Her tears at the time had moved neither of them. That was the way of it. And if late at night, lying by the unmoving mound of her husband, she dreamed of green meadows and a child touched by the wind, it was a fancy spun into an unheeding night. There were no meadows, no green, no child.

Her life was bounded by her husband and her house. There was a hardscrabble garden she tended with little success. Only occasionally would brown plants push throught the slate, their roots digging shallow graves in the pumice. And Cybele clung, like tender moss, to the outer edge of the man of stone.

All she had ever wanted was a child, but she had dared ask only twice before his silence and his anger overwhelmed her wish.

The first time she asked was the night they were married. Her hand had been transferred from father to husband before the cold eye of the celibate priest. Craig's hand was hard in hers, the knuckles on it rose like hills of flint. She had put her mouth on those hills to quicken them. She looked up at him, her eyes brimming over. "Will we make a child tonight?" she had wondered aloud, a bridal wish.

"No child," he growled. "I'll have no child." It was a statement, not a guess.

Months later, when she knew him and had only started to fade into hopelessness, she had tried again.

"With a child between us," she began.

But he gnawed at the words. "No child."

So the years were all that they shared between them; and sorrow was all she bore.

There might never have been a third time if a false spring had not brought a gentle wind to their house. Cybele startled a brown bird off its nest. There were two small greying eggs. The bird did not return, and so finally, fearfully, she brought the eggs inside and tried to hatch them near the fire. But the eggs turned cold before the day's end. She cracked the eggs open and found the unborn chicks inside, their dead bodies only partially formed. Blind membraned eyes seemed to stare up at her. She buried them under a stone in the garden, afraid she might otherwise have to feed them to Craig.

But she dreamed of the birds in her sleep and cried out: "The children."

It woke Craig, and he in turn woke her.

They sat up in the bed, staring at one another in the half-light of dawn. "Children?" he asked. "What children?"

"It was a dream," she replied.

"I said there would be no children," Craig said, his voice rising to a shout.

She shrugged and turned from him. "A stone cannot make a child."

"You scorn the stone? The stone that gives me a living? The stone that gives us a life?"

Her back to him, she lay down again and said "I do not

scorn the stone that is your work, but *you* who are stone instead of man. And a man of stone cannot make a child."

"You think I am incapable of making a child? I *shall* make one," he said, leaping out of the bed. "But not with you. No, I shall make a child of stone." He dressed himself in silence, picked up his tools, and went from the house.

The silence after his leaving struck Cybele like a blow. She had never heard so many words from him at one time. She had never spoken so many in return. She feared her words had damaged him beyond healing, had shattered something inside him that would not come right again. She dressed in the darkness of the house and went outside into the dawn.

She had never been to the quarry before. Indeed she was not even sure of the way. Craig had made it clear that the quarry was his and the house hers. But she followed a path she had often seen him take and came within minutes to the place where he worked.

The quarry was lit by both the setting moon and the rising sun. No shadows yet marked its face. It stood waiting for the touch of Craig's hammer, waiting to submit to each blow.

Craig had set to work at once. His first angry strokes had been so quick, they seemed random, unplanned, a cleaving of rock and rock. But as his anger drained from him and his body took up the rhythm of his work again, a rough shape began to emerge from the quarry wall.

He had thought to make a child of stone, but the hammer had chosen differently. In all his life he had never really looked at a child, so the form that came from the stone was as tall as a man and as broad.

Once the form was wrested from the rock, Craig took out

his finer chisels. Using his own body as a model, he shaped each nail, each muscle, each hair in the rock. Only the face he left blank.

The sun traveled overhead. His wife watched silently, unheeded, by a tree at the quarry's edge.

Craig worked without stopping, shaping the rock to his will. He breathed heavily, and the rock dust swirled about him, rising and falling with each breath.

The sun struck its zenith and went down. Craig wiped the sweat from his eyes, felt the sweat running down his arms and legs, collecting in his body's cracks, and pooling in his hair.

Before him the man of rock stood faceless but otherwise complete. Only one cord of rock attached the figure to the quarry's side.

Craig stood tall, the hammer in his hand. He drew in a deep breath and threw out his chest. His lungs ached with the effort. He felt a wild exaltation. With a cry, he brought the hammer full force on the fragile link between rock and rock.

"*Aieee,*" he called, "my son!"

The faceless man of rock shuddered with the releasing blow. It seemed as if the figure itself might shatter.

Craig shook his head free of the sweat which clouded his eyes. Drops spattered the rock form. It stumbled forward, caught itself, stood upright, then turned its blank face towards Craig. It raised its arms in supplication.

The movement frightened Craig. He was not prepared for it. He raised the hammer once again, this time to shatter the man of rock.

"Oh, no," cried Cybele from the quarry's edge. "He is your son."

Craig turned at the sound, and the man of rock reached out and wrested the hammer from his grasp. With a silent shout it brought the hammer down.

Craig fell, face into the earth, and lay like a pile of jumbled stones.

The man of rock stood still for a moment. Then he turned his head toward the sky, blindly seeking light. The risen moon cast shadowy features on his face. Raising his fingers to his head, the man of rock engraved those shadows onto the blank: eyes, nose, a firm slash of mouth. Then he bent over and picked up the rest of Craig's tools. When he straightened again, he looked over at the piles of stones, crumpled and unmoving on the quarry floor.

"*Aieee,* my father," he whispered into the silence. In his new eyes were the beginnings of tears.

He turned and saw Cybele, standing on the path. "Mother?" he asked. She said nothing, but smiled, and that smile drew him surely into her waiting arms.

As the woman listened to the dream, her hand smoothed the sides of her dress with long strokes. At dream's end, she looked up at her husband and tried to reach his eyes with hers. A smile trembled uncertainly on her lips.

He looked for a moment down at her: then his eyes slid away from hers. "You can't mean you believe such childish tales? There is no

29

man, no woman, no rock, no stone. There is no truth in it. It was a waste of time, and time is the only truth in this world that one can be sure of. Come, we are late." He held out his arm.

Hand upon arm, they walked up the steps toward the Great Temple and left the dream behind.

Hearing them go, the Dream Weaver shook her head. She finished off the dream and put in the bag. The morning sun was warm on her face. She folded her hands before her and almost slept.

"I want a dream!" The voice was a man's, harsh and insistent. She had heard it many times before, but in her half-sleep his remembered footsteps had merged with the sounds of the day. "I have your money, old woman. Give me a good one."

"Just a penny," said the Dream Weaver, rousing herself.

"It is a five-penny piece," said the man. "For that I expect something special."

The Weaver sighed. The man came nearly every week with the same request. Five pennies for a one-penny dream. Yet he was never happy with the result. She pulled new threads from her basket and began.

In a village that sat well back in a quiet valley, there lived an old woman and the last of her seven sons. The others had gone to join the army as they came of age, and the only one left at home was a lad named Karl.

Even if he had not been her last, his mother would have loved him best for he had a sweet disposition and a sweeter voice. It was because of that voice, pure and clear, that caroled like spring birds, that she had called him Karel. But his brothers, fearing the song name would unman him, had changed it to Karl. So Karl he had remained.

"No," said the man harshly. "I do not like it. I can see already it is not the dream for me. I am no singer, no minstrel. I am a man of consequence."

"But you must wait until it is done," said the Dream Weaver. "Dreams are not finished until the very end. They change. They flow. They have undercurrents. Perhaps it is not a story about singing at all. How can you know?"

"I know enough," said the man. "I do not want to hear more."

The Dream Weaver felt the wool snarl under her fingers. She sighed.

"I would have given five pennies for a good dream," said the man. "But that is only the smallest part of a dream, and not a good dream at that." He threw a small coin at the Dream Weaver's feet.

"It is enough," said the old woman, finding the penny with her fingers. And then, to the man's back as his footsteps hurried away from her, she added, "Enough for me. But what is enough for you?" She finished off the fragment with knowing fingers and put it with the others in her pack.

She stretched then, carefully, but did not arise. It was a good place that she had, by the steps. People passed it all the time. She did not want someone else to take it.

Raising her face to the sun, she would have fallen into that half sleep which age so easily granted her, when a sound down the walkway stopped her. She put her hand out again and took up her call: "A penny, a penny, a penny for a dream."

A young woman, tall and slim, dressed in black, came slowly toward the steps. She held a child by the hand. As they neared the Dream Weaver, the old woman called out again, "A penny for a dream."

The child, also in black, strained at his mother's hand. At the

31

Dream Weaver's call, he turned in surprise to look up at his mother. "You said all the dreams were dead. How can they be if this granny can make a new one? And just for a penny."

"Child," his mother began painfully. Her hand moved her black veil aside, and she looked at the Dream Weaver with swollen eyes. Dropping the veil again, she repeated, "Child."

"But I have a penny, Mother. Here." The child's hand dug into his pocket and emerged with a sticky coin. "Please."

The veiled head looked down, shook slowly once, twice; but still the woman took the coin. Handing it to the Dream Weaver cautiously, she said, "Weave us a dream, granny, for the boy and me. But I pray that it is a gentle one, full of loving."

The Dream Weaver took the coin, making it disappear in her robes. Then she settled herself to the task. Her hands flew over the loom, and she plucked the strings as if she were a musician, her fingers gentle yet strong. And this was the dream that she wove.

❧ The Tree's Wife ❧

There was once a young woman named Drusilla who had been widowed longer than she was wed. She had been married at fifteen to a rich old man who beat her. She had flowered despite his ill treatment, and it was he who died, within the year, leaving her all alone in the great house.

Once the old man was dead, his young widow was courted by many, for she was now quite wealthy. The young men came together, and all claimed that she needed a husband to help her.

But Drusilla would have none of them. "When I was

poor," she said, "not one of you courted me. When I was ill treated, not one of you stood by me. I never asked for more than a gentle word, yet I never received one. So now that you ask, I will have none of you."

She turned her back on them, then stopped. She looked around at the grove of birch trees by her house. "Why, I would sooner wed this tree," she said, touching a sturdy birch that stood to one side, "A tree would know when to bend and when to stand. I would sooner wed this tree than marry another man."

At that very moment, a passing wind caused the top branches of the birch to sway.

The rejected suitors laughed at Drusilla. "See," they jeered, "the tree has accepted your offer."

And so she was known from that day as the Tree's Wife.

To keep the jest from hurting, Drusilla entered into it with a will. If someone came to the house, she would put her arms around the birch, caressing its bark and stroking its limbs.

"I have all I need or want with my tree," she would say. And her laugh was a silent one back at the stares. She knew that nothing confounds jokers as much as madness, so she made herself seem very mad for them.

But madness also makes folk uneasy; they fear contagion. And soon Drusilla found herself quite alone. Since it was not of her choosing, the aloneness began to gnaw at her. It was true that what she really wanted was just a kind word, but soon she was so lonely almost any word would have done.

So it happened one night, when the moon hung in the sky like a ripe yellow apple, that a wind blew fiercely from the north. It made the trees bow and bend and knock their

branches against Drusilla's house. Hearing them knock, she looked out of the windows and saw the trees dancing wildly in the wind.

They seemed to beckon and call, and she was suddenly caught up in their rhythm. She swayed with them, but it was not enough. She longed for the touch of the wind on her skin, so she ran outside, leaving the door ajar. She raised her hands above her head and danced with the trees.

In the darkness, surrounded by the shadow of its brothers, one tree seemed to shine. It was her tree, the one she had chosen. It was touched with a phosphorescent glow, and the vein of each leaf was a streak of pale fire.

Drusilla danced over to the tree and held her hands toward it. "Oh, if only you *were* a man, or I a tree," she said out loud. "If you were a man tall and straight and gentle and strong then—yes—then I would be happy."

The wind died as suddenly as it had begun, and the trees stood still. Drusilla dropped her hands, feeling foolish and shamed, but a movement in the white birch stayed her. As she watched, it seemed to her that first two legs, then a body, then a head and arms emerged from the bark; a shadowy image pulling itself painfully free of the trunk. The image shimmered for a moment, trembled, and then became clear. Before her stood a man.

He was tall and slim, with skin as white as the bark of the birch and hair as black as the birch bark patches. His legs were strong yet supple, and his feet were knotty and tapered like roots. His hands were thin and veined with green, and the second and third fingers grew together, slotted like a leaf. He smiled at her and held out his arms, an echo of her earlier plea,

35

and his arms swayed up and down as if touched by a passing breeze.

Drusilla stood without movement, without breath. Then he nodded his head, and she went into his arms. When his mouth came down on hers, she smelled the damp woody odor of his breath.

They lay together all night below his tree, cradled in its roots. But when the sun began its climb against the furthest hills, the man pulled himself reluctantly from Drusilla's arms and disappeared back into the tree.

Call as she might, Drusilla could not bring him out again, but one of the tree branches reached down and stroked her arm in a lover's farewell.

She spent the next days under the tree, reading and weaving and playing her lute. And the tree itself seemed to listen and respond. The branches touched and turned the pages of her book. The whole tree moved to the beauty of her songs.

Yet it was not until the next full moon that the man could pull himself from the tree and sleep away the dark in her arms.

Still Drusilla was content. For as she grew in her love for the man of the tree, her love for all nature grew, a quiet pullulation. She felt kin to every flower and leaf. She heard the silent speech of the green world and, under the bark, the beating of each heart.

One day, when she ventured into the village, Drusilla's neighbors observed that she was growing more beautiful in her madness. The boldest of them, an old woman, asked, "If you have no man, how is it you bloom?"

Drusilla turned to look at the old woman and smiled. It was a slow smile. "I am the tree's wife," she said, "in truth.

And he is man enough for me." It was all the answer she would return.

But in the seventh month since the night of the apple moon, Drusilla knew she carried a child, the tree's child, below her heart. And when she told the tree of it, its branches bent around her and touched her hair. And when she told the man of it, he smiled and held her gently.

Drusilla wondered what the child would be that rooted in her. She wondered if it would burgeon into a human child or emerge some great wooden beast. Perhaps it would be both, with arms and legs as strong as the birch and leaves for hair. She feared her heart would burst with the questions. But on the next full moon, the tree man held her and whispered in her ear such soft, caressing sounds, she grew calm. And at last she knew that however the child grew, she would love it. And with that knowledge she was once again content.

Soon it was evident, even to the townsfolk, that she blossomed with child. They looked for the father among themselves—for where else *could* they look—but no one admitted to the deed. And Drusilla herself would name no one but the tree to midwife, priest, or mayor.

And so, where at first the villagers had jested at her and joked with her and felt themselves plagued by her madness, now they turned wicked and cruel. They could accept a widow's madness but not a mother unwed.

The young men, the late suitors, pressed on by the town elders, came to Drusilla one night. In the darkness, they would have pulled her from her house and beaten her. But Drusilla heard them come and climbed through the window and fled to the top of the birch.

The wind raged so that night that the branches of the tree flailed like whips, and not one of the young men dared come close enough to climb the tree and take Drusilla down. All they could do was try and wound her with their words. They shouted up at her where she sat near the top of the birch, cradled in its branches. But she did not hear their shouts. She was lulled instead by the great rustling voices of the grove.

In the morning the young men were gone. They did not return.

And Drusilla did not go back into the town. As the days passed, she was fed by the forest and the field. Fruits and berries and sweet sap found their way to her doorstep. Each morning she had enough for the day. She did not ask where it all came from, but still she knew.

At last it was time for the child to be born. On this night of a full moon, Drusilla's pains began. Holding her sides with slender fingers, she went out to the base of the birch, sat down, and leaned her back against the tree, straining to let the child out. As she pushed, the birch man pulled himself silently from the tree, knelt by her, and breathed encouragements into her face. He stroked her hair and whispered her name to the wind.

She did not smile up at him but said at last, "Go." Her breath was ragged and her voice on the edge of despair. "I beg you. Get the midwife. This does not go well."

The tree man held her close, but he did not rise.

"Go," she begged. "Tell her my name. It is time."

He took her face in his hands and stared long into it with his woods-green eyes. He pursed his lips as if to speak, then stood up and was gone.

He went down the path towards the town, though each step away from the tree drew his strength from him. Patches of skin peeled off as he moved, and the sores beneath were dark and viscous. His limbs grew more brittle with each step, and he moved haltingly. By the time he reached the midwife's house, he looked an aged and broken thing. He knocked upon the door, yet he was so weak, it was only a light tapping, a scraping, the scratching of a branch across a window pane.

As if she had been waiting for his a call, the midwife came at once. She opened the door and stared at what stood before her. Tall and thin and naked and white, with black patches of scabrous skin and hair as dark as rotting leaves, the tree man held up his grotesque, slotted hand. The gash of his mouth was hollow and tongueless, a sap-filled wound. He made no sound, but the midwife screamed and screamed, and screaming still, slammed the door.

She did not see him fall.

In the morning the townsfolk came to Drusilla's great house. They came armed with clubs and cudgels and forks. The old midwife was in the rear, calling the way.

Beneath a dead white tree they found Drusilla, pale and barely moving, a child cradled in her arms. At the townsfolk's coming, the child opened its eyes. They were the color of winter pine.

"Poor thing," said the midwife, stepping in front of the men. "I knew no good would come of this." She bent to take the child from Drusilla's arms but leaped up again with a cry. For the child had uncurled one tiny fist, and its hand was veined with green and the second and third fingers grew together, slotted like a leaf.

At the midwife's cry, the birches in the grove began to move and sway, though there was not a breath of breeze. And before any weapon could be raised, the nearest birch stretched its branches far out and lifted the child and Drusilla up, up towards the top of the tree.

As the townsfolk watched, Drusilla disappeared. The child seemed to linger for a moment longer, its unclothed body gleaming in the sun. Then slowly the child faded, like melting snow on pine needles, like the last white star of morning, into the heart of the tree.

There was a soughing as of wind through branches, a tremble of leaves, and one sharp cry of an unsuckled child. Then the trees in the grove were still.

"*Thank you," said the widow softly. She patted the Dream Weaver's shoulder. Then she spoke to her child, "Come. We will go to your father's people. They will take us in, I know that now." She held out her hand.*

The child took her hand, and as they began walking, he asked, "Did you like it? Was it a good dream? I thought it was sad. Was it sad?"

But his mother did not answer him, and soon the child's voice, like their footsteps, faded away.

The Dream Weaver took the dream from the loom. "They, too, left without the dream. Such a small bit of weaving, yet they had no room for it. But it was not a sad dream. Not really. It had much loving in it. She should have taken it for the child—if not for herself." And still mumbling, the Dream Weaver snipped the threads and finished off the weaving, stretching it a bit to make it more pliant. Then she put it, with the others, in her bag.

"Dream Weaver" came a chorus of voices. The Dream Weaver sorted out three. Three children. Girls, she thought.

The boldest of the three, the middle child, stepped closer. All three were tawny-haired, though the oldest had curls with an orange tinge to them. "Dream Weaver, we have only one penny to spend. One for the three of us. Can you weave us one dream? To share?"

"Share a dream?" The old woman laughed. "It is the best way. Of course you can share. Are you . . . ." she hesitated, then guessed, "sisters?"

"How can she tell?" whispered the youngest.

"Hush," cautioned the middle child. "Manners!"

The oldest ignored them. On the edge of womanhood, she was aware of urges in herself she could not yet name. She gathered her skirts and her courage, and squatted down by the weaver. "Could you," she began tentatively, "could you put true love in it?"

The Dream Weaver smiled. She had heard such requests many times over. But she would never have convinced the girl of that. Better to let the child think she was the only one with such a dream.

"Oh, true love!" said the middle child. "That's all you ever think about—now. You used to be fun."

The youngest girl lisped. "A cat, please, granny. Please let there be a cat in it."

"A cat! True love! I only want it to be fun. For the penny we should have a good laugh," the middle child said.

The Dream Weaver smiled again as she pulled the threads from her basket. "Well, we shall see, little ones. A cat and true love and a laugh. I have had stranger demands. But one never knows about a dream until it is done. Still, I will try. And since it is your dream, you each must try as well."

"Try?" the three exclaimed as one. And the youngest added, "How shall we try, granny?"

"Hold hands, and I shall weave. And as I weave, you must believe."

"Oh, we will," said the youngest breathlessly. The other two laughed at her, but they held hands. The warp was strung. The weaver began.

❧ The Cat Bride ❧

There was once a noddy old woman who had only two things in the world that she loved—her son and a marmalade cat. She loved them both the same, which seemed strange to her neighbors but not to her son, Tom.

"I bring home food, and the cat keeps it safe. Why should we not share equally in her affections?" he asked sensibly. Then he added, "Though I am not the best provider in the land, the cat is surely the best mouser. *Ergo,* it follows."

But of course it did not follow for the neighbors. To them

such sense was nonsense. However, as it was none of their business, the old woman ignored their mischievous tongues and loved boy and cat the same.

One day the old woman caught a chill, grew sicker, and likened to die. She called Tom and the cat to her bed. The village elders came, too, for they went to deathbeds as cats to mackerel; the smell, it was said, drew them in.

"Promise me, Tom," said the old woman in a voice as soft as down.

"Anything, Mother," said Tom as he sat by her bed and held on to her hand.

"Promise me you will marry the marmalade cat, for that way she will remain in our family forever. You are a good boy, Tom, but she is the best mouser in the land."

At her words, the elders cried out to one another in horror.

"Never," cried one.

"Unheard of," cried the second.

"It is against the law," declared the third.

"What law?" asked the old woman, looking over at them. "Where is it written that a boy cannot marry a cat?"

The elders looked at one another. They twisted their mouths around, but no answer came out, for she was right.

"I promise, Mother," said Tom, "for I love the marmalade cat as much as you do. I will keep her safe and in our family forever."

As soon as Tom had finished speaking, the cat jumped onto the bed and, as if to seal its part of the bargain, licked the old woman's face, first one cheek and then the other, with its rough-ribbed tongue. Then it bit her softly on the nose and jumped down.

At the cat's touch, the elders left the room in disgust. But the old woman sat up in bed. Color sprang into her faded cheeks, and she let out a high sweet laugh.

Tom's heart sang out a silent hallelujah. He rose to shut the door. When he turned back again, there was an orange-haired girl with green eyes standing where the cat had been, but the cat was nowhere in sight.

"Who are you, and where is the cat?" asked Tom.

"Why, I *am* the cat," said the girl. "But if we are to be wed, it is best that I wear human clothes."

"I liked you well enough before," said Tom, looking at the floor.

"Well, you will like her well enough after," said his mother sensibly. She got out of bed, toddled to the door, and called out to the village elders who were already more than halfway down the road.

Smelling a miracle, the elders turned back. And though they did not like it all the way through, they agreed to marry Tom and the girl at once. "For," said one to the others, "a girl with orange hair and green eyes and the manners of a cat should not be left to wander the village on her own."

Several days went by before the elders returned for a visit.

"We are glad to see you are still well," the first said to the old woman as she sat and nodded by the fire.

"Some miracles are but a moment long," said the second. He tried not to stare at Tom's new wife who lay dozing on the hearth, her skirts tucked up around her long slim legs.

But the third leaned closer to the old woman and whispered in her ear. "I have been wanting to ask—how is she as a bride?"

45

"Cat or girl, I love her still with all my heart," said the old woman. "And she is the perfect girl for Tom. She is neat and clean. She is quick on her feet. She has a warm and loving heart."

"Well," said the third elder, twisting his mouth around the word, "I suppose *that* is good."

"Well," said the old woman, smiling up at him "if that were all, it would be good enough. But there is even better."

"Better?" asked the elder.

"Better," said the old woman with a mischievous grin. "She is neat and clean and quick on her feet and has a warm and loving heart. And," she paused, "she is still the best mouser in the land."

The three girls laughed their thanks and walked away, chattering. They left the dream behind.

The Weaver began to remove the dream when angry steps caused her to pause.

"You again," she said.

"It might not be a minstrel's dream. You said that. So, for the coin I gave you already, finish the dream."

"I cannot finish that one," said the Dream Weaver. "The fragment is already packed away."

"Do not try to wheedle another penny from me," the man shouted. He moved as if to turn away.

The Dream Weaver shook her head. "I want no more from you," she said, "though I would not turn down another penny."

"Here," he said, and threw a coin at her feet.

The Dream Weaver found it and tucked it away, then added, "I will pick threads that are close to the first ones. But they might not be a match. Will you stay through this time and listen to your dream?"

The man grunted his answer and watched as the old woman finished off the girls' dream and rummaged in her thread basket. She pulled out several.

"How can you be sure those are near the color of the last when you cannot see?" asked the man.

The Dream Weaver was silent as she finished sorting the threads. "Well?"

"By the feel, man. Just as I can tell, from your voice, the look of your face, though I have no eyes."

"And what is that look?" he asked.

"My answer would not flatter you!" she said. "So hush, for the dream is beginning." She threaded the warp and began.

❧ The Boy Who Sang for Death ❧

In a village that lay like a smudge on the cheek of a quiet valley, there lived an old woman and the last of her seven sons. The oldest six had joined the army as they came of age, and her husband was long in his grave. The only one left at home was a lad named Karl.

Even if he had not been her last, his mother would have

loved him best for he had a sweet disposition and a sweeter voice. It was because of that voice, pure and clear, that caroled like spring birds, that she had called him Karel. But his father and brothers, fearing the song name would unman him, had changed it to Karl. So Karl he had remained.

Karl was a sturdy boy, a farm boy in face and hands. But his voice set him apart from the rest. Untutored and untrained, Karl's voice could call home sheep from the pasture, birds from the trees. In the village, it was even said that the sound of Karl's voice made graybeards dance, the lame to walk, and milk spring from a maiden's breast. Yet Karl used his voice for no such magic, but to please his mother and gentle his flock.

On day when Karl was out singing to the sheep and goats to bring them safely in from the field, his voice broke; like a piece of cloth caught on a nail, it tore. Fearing something wrong at home, he hurried the beasts. They scattered before him, and he came to the house to find that this mother had died.

"Between one breath and the next, she was gone," said the priest.

Gently Karl folded her hands on her breast and, although she was beyond the sound of his song, he whispered something in her ear and turned to leave.

"Where are you going?" called out the priest, his words heavy with concern.

"I am going to find Death and bring my mother back," cried Karl, his jagged voice now dulled with grief. He turned at the door and faced the priest who knelt by his mother's bed. "Surely Death will accept an exchange. What is one old tired woman to Death who has known so many?"

"And will you recognize Death, my son, when you meet him?"

"That I do not know," said Karl.

The priest nodded and rose heavily from his knees. "Then listen well, my son. Death is an aging but still handsome prince. His eyes are dark and empty for he has seen much suffering in the world. If you find such a one, he is Death."

"I will know him," said Karl.

"And what can you give Death in exchange that he has not already had many times over?" asked the priest.

Karl touched his pockets and sighed. "I have nothing here to give," he said. "But I hope that he may listen to my songs. They tell me in the village that there is a gift of magic in my voice. Any gift I have I would surely give to get my mother back. I will sing for Death, and perhaps that great prince will take time to listen."

"Death does not take time," said the old priest, raising his hand to bless the boy, "for time is Death's own greatest possession."

"I can but try," said Karl, tears in his eyes. He knelt a moment for the blessing, stood up and went out the door. He did not look back.

Karl walked for many days and came at last to a city that lay like a blemish on three hills. He listened quietly but well, as only a singer can, and when he heard weeping, he followed the sound and found a funeral procession bearing the coffin of a child. The procession turned into a graveyard where stones leaned upon stones like cards in a neglected deck.

"Has Death been here already?" asked Karl of a weeping woman.

"Death has been here many times," she answered. "But today she has taken my child."

"*She?*" said Karl. "But surely Death is a man."

"Death is a woman," she answered him at once. "Her hair is long and thick and dark, like the roots of trees. Her body is huge and brown, but she is barren. The only way she can bear a child is to bear it away."

Karl felt her anger and sorrow then, for they matched his own, so he joined the line of mourners to the grave. And when the child's tiny box had been laid in the ground, he sang it down with the others. But his voice lifted above theirs, a small bird soaring with ease over larger ones. The townsfolk stopped singing in amazement and listened to him.

Karl sang not of Death but of his village in the valley, of the seasons that sometime stumble one into another, and of the small pleasures of the hearth. He sang tune after tune the whole of that day, and just at nightfall he stopped. They threw dirt on the baby's coffin and brought Karl to their home.

"Your songs eased my little one's passage," said the woman. "Stay with us this night. We owe you that,"

"I wish that I had been here before," said Karl. "I might have saved your baby with a song."

"I fear Death would not be cheated so easily of her chosen child," said the woman. She set the table but did not eat.

Karl left in the morning. And as he walked, he thought about Death, how it was a hollow-eyed prince to the priest but a jealous mother to the woman. If Death could change shapes with such ease, how would he know Death when they finally met? He walked and walked, his mind in a puzzle, until he came at last to a plain that lay like a great open wound between mountains.

The plain was filled with an army of fighting men. There were men with bows and men with swords and men with wooden staves. Some men fought on horseback, and some fought from their knees. Karl could not tell one band of men from another, could not match friend with friend, foe with foe, for their clothes were colored by dirt and by blood and every man looked the same. And the screams and shouts and the crying of horns were a horrible symphony in Karl's ears.

Yet there was one figure Karl *could* distinguish. A woman, quite young, dressed in a long white gown. Her dark braids were caught up in ribbons of white and looped like a crown on her head. She threaded her way through the ranks of men like a shuttle through a loom, and there seemed to be a pattern in her going. She paused now and then to put a hand to the head or the breast of one man and then another. Each man she touched stopped fighting and, with an expression of surprise, left his body and followed the girl, so that soon there was a great wavering line of grey men trailing behind her.

Then Karl knew that he had found Death.

He ran down the mountainside and around the flank of the great plain, for he wanted to come upon Death face to face. He called out as he ran, hoping to slow her progress, "Wait, oh, wait, my Lady Death; please wait for me."

Lady Death heard his call above the battle noise, and she looked up from her work. A weariness sat between her eyes, but she did not stop. She continued her way from man to man, a hand to the brow or over the heart. And at her touch, each man left his life to follow the young girl named Death.

When Karl saw that she would not stop at his calling, he stepped into her path. But she walked through him as if through air and went on her way, threading the line of dead grey men behind her.

So Karl began to sing. It was all he knew to do.

He sang not of death but of growing and bearing, for they were things she knew nothing of. He sang of small birds on the apple spray and bees with their honeyed burden. He sang of the first green blades piercing the warmed earth. He sang of winter fields where moles and mice sleep quietly under the snow. Each tune swelled into the next.

And Lady Death stopped to listen.

As she stopped, the ribbon of soldiers that was woven behind her stopped, too, and from their dead eyes tears fell with each memory. The battlefield was still, frozen by the songs. And the only sound and the only movement and the only breath was Karl's voice.

When he had finished at last, a tiny brown bird flew out of a dead tree, took up the last melody, and went on.

"I have made you stop, Lady Death," cried Karl. "And you have listened to my tunes. Will you now pay for that pleasure?"

Lady Death smiled, a slow, weary smile, and Karl wondered that someone so young should have to carry such a burden. And his pity hovered between them in the quiet air.

"I will pay, Karel," she said.

He did not wonder that she knew his true name, for Lady Death would, in the end, know every human's name.

"Then I ask for my mother in exchange," said Karl.

Lady Death looked at him softly then. She took up his pity

and gave it back. "That I cannot do. Who follows me once, follows forever. But is it not payment enough to know that you have stayed my hand for this hour? No man has ever done that before."

"But you promised to pay," said Karl. His voice held both anger and disappointment, a man and a child's voice in one.

"And what I promise," she said, looking at him from under darkened lids, "I do."

The Dream Weaver's voice stopped for a moment.

"Is that all?" asked the man. "That is no ending. What of the coins I gave you?"

"Hush," the Dream Weaver said to him. "This is strange. This has never happened before. There is not one ending but two. I feel that here," and she held up her hands.

"Then tell them to me. Both. I paid," he said.

The Dream Weaver nodded. "This is the first way the dream ends," she said, and wove.

Lady Death put her hand in front of her, as if reaching into a cupboard, and a grey form that was strangely transparent took shape under her fingers. It became a harp, with smoke-colored strings the color of Lady Death's eyes.

"A useless gift," said Karl. "I cannot play."

But Lady Death reached over and set the harp in his hand, careful not to touch him with her own.

And as the harp molded itself under his fingers, Karl felt music surge through his bones. He put his thumb and fore-finger on the strings and began to play.

At the first note, the battle began anew. Men fought, men bled, men suffered, men fell. But Karl passed through the armies untouched, playing a sweet tune that rose upward, in bursts, as the lark and its song spring toward the sun. He walked through the armies, through the battle, through the plain, playing his harp, and he never looked back again.

The Dream Weaver hesitated but a moment.
"And the other ending," the man commanded.
But she had already begun.

"And what I promise," Death said, looking at him from under darkened lids, "I do."

She turned and pointed to the field, and Karl's eyes followed her fingers.

"There in that field are six men whose heads and hearts I will not touch this day. Look carefully, Karl."

He looked. "They are my brothers," he said.

"Them, I will spare." And Lady Death turned and stared into Karl's face with her smoky eyes. "But I would have you sing for me again each night in the small hours when I rest, for I have never had such comfort before. Will you come?" She held out her hand.

Karl hesitated a moment, remembering his farm, remembering the fields, the valleys, the warm spring rains. Then he looked again at Lady Death, whose smile seemed a little less weary. He nodded and reached for her hand, and it was small and soft and cool in his. He raised her hand once to his lips, then set it, palm open, over his heart. He never felt the cold.

Then, hand in hand, Karl and Lady Death walked through the battlefield. Their passing made not even the slightest breeze on the cheeks of the wounded, nor an extra breath for the dying. Only the dead who traveled behind saw them pass under the shadows of the farthest hills. But long after they had gone, the little bird sang Karl's last song over and over and over again into the darkening air.

"I liked the other ending best," said the man. "It was the better bargain."

"Bargain?" The Dream Weaver's mouth soured with the word.

"A bargain, old one," he said. "The boy bought a salable talent with his song. He got better than he gave and that is always a bargain. I like that." The man chuckled to himself and went away, his footsteps tapping lightly on the street.

"A bargain was it?" the Weaver mumbled to herself, finishing off the tale and its two separate endings. "A bargain!" she said again, shaking her head. She thought for a moment of taking the first ending apart, saving the threads for another time. She knew the man would not be back for it, and it had not pleased her, that ending. Still, she could not bear to unravel her work, so she put it with the others in her bag.

The Dream Weaver fingered the coins in her pouch. Five already, no, six, and the sun was on its downward swing. It had been a good day. She could begin her slow dark trip home.

"There she is, the Dream Weaver," came a voice. "Stop her. Oh, stop!"

The Dream Weaver, half standing, heard the voice and running steps as one. She turned and waited. Another coin to put in the pouch, to hold against the rains or the long, cold winter days.

"You are not through, Dream Weaver?" It was a young voice, a girl just become a woman. She sounded only slightly worried, stuttering a bit from the run.

"No, child, not if you want a dream."

"We want a dream. Together, Dream Weaver." It was almost a man's voice, just out of boyhood but already gone through its change. "We made our pledges to one another today. We will be married by year's end. We have saved a coin to celebrate our fortune and we have decided together on a dream. Give us a good one."

The old woman smiled. "I have already spun one true love dream today. I do not know if there is another in these old fingers." She held them up before her eyes as if she could see them. She was proud of them, her clever fingers. She knew that they were strong and supple despite their gnarled appearance.

"Oh, we do not need a true love dream," came the girl's quick response. "We have that ourselves, you see. Our parents would have married us to others—for gold. But we persuaded them to let us wed. It took a long time, too long. But . . ." She stopped as if to let the boy finish for her, but he was silent, simply staring at her while she spoke.

"Well, give me the coin then, and we shall see what the threads have to say," said the Dream Weaver. "They never lie. But sometimes the dream is not easy to read."

The young man handed her the coin, and she slipped it into the pouch. She heard not even a rustle of impatience. They simply waited for her to begin, confident in their own living dreams.

The Dream Weaver picked out the threads with more flourish than was necessary. She would give them their penny's worth.

"Watch as I thread the warp," commanded the Dream Weaver, knowing they might need prompting to look at her rather than at one another.

At her command, they turned to watch. And this was the dream that she wove.

❧ Princess Heart O'Stone ❧

In the days when woods still circled the world and heroes could talk with beasts, there lived a princess whom everyone pitied.

She was the most beautiful girl imaginable. Her hair was the color of red leaves in the fall, burnished with orange and gold. Her eyes were the green of moss on stone, and her skin the color of fresh cream. She was slim and fair, and her voice was low. But she had a heart of stone.

When she was born, the midwife had grasped her firmly and slapped her lightly to bring out the first cry. But the first cry was the midwife's instead.

"Look!" the woman gasped, pointing to the child's breast. And there, cold and unmoving under the fragile shield of skin, was the outline of a heart. "She has a heart of stone."

Then the child made a sound that was neither laugh nor cry and opened her eyes, but the stone in her breast did not move at all.

The king put his right palm on the child's body, nearly covering it. He shook his head.

The queen turned her face against the pillow, but she could not weep until she heard the king weep. Then they wept as one.

The midwife was paid twice over in gold to stop her tongue, but it was too late. Her cry had already been heard. It went round the castle before the child had been wrapped.

"The princess has a heart of stone."

"The princess has a heart of stone."

The child grew up, hearing the whispers. And knowing her heart was made of stone and could feel neither sorrow nor joy, she felt nothing. She accepted the friendship of birds and beasts who asked neither smiles nor tears of her but only the comfort of her hand. But she stayed aloof from the companionship of people. And that is why she was called Princess Heart O'Stone—and was pitied.

Her parents would have done anything for her, but what could they do? They called in physicians who examined her. They thumped her bones and pulled at her skin and looked at her ears and eyes. They gave advice and said what was already known. "She is perfectly fit, except—except that her heart is made of stone."

The king and queen called in poets and painters and singers of songs. They told of love never plighted, of wars never won, of mothers whose children all died.

The princess did not cry.

"If we can not move her, nothing can," they said, and left.

The royal couple called in clowns. And the courtyards of the kingdom filled with jongleurs and jesters, jugglers and jokers, who fell over one another in their efforts to fill the princess with delight. But as she had never cried, so she never laughed.

61

"What a heartless creature," said the clowns. And they went away.

At last the king and queen gave up hope for a cure. Indeed they had lived through so many false promises and so much useless advice that they declared no one was ever again to speak of changing the princess' condition. To do so was to invite a beheading.

Now in that same kingdom lived a simple woodcutter whose name was Donnal.

As fair as the princess was, Donnal was fairer. He had an angel's face set round with golden curls. He was tall and straight, and his heart was tender. If he had a fault, it was this: he was proud of his strong back and perfect limbs and liked to admire his image in the forest pools.

Now one day, deep in the woods where he worked, Donnal heard a faint cry. As he knew the songs of birds, he ran to the sound and there he found a sparrow hawk caught in a net. Donnal took out his knife and cut the bird free. It flew straight to a low branch and called its thanks to the lad:

Heart O'Stone
Is all alone.

"Well, that is strange thanks, indeed," thought Donnal. But the call stayed with him all that day. And as he thought about it, his tender heart cried out with pity. Though he lived in the woods by himself, *he* was not alone. He had all the birds and beasts and his own fair reflection for company. He could enjoy them and laugh or cry at will. But the princess, fair and stone-hearted, was truly all alone.

Still it did not occur to Donnal to go to her. He was a woodcutter, after all. How could he presume to help her when physicians and poets and clowns could not?

The very next day, when Donnal was again hard at work, he heard a second cry. It was deeper than the voice of the bird. Donnal ran to it and found a small vixen caught in a trap. He bent down and opened the trap and the little fox ran free. She cowered for a moment under a bush and, in thanks, barked:

> Carry her heart,
> Never part.

"Well," said Donnal, "that is certainly true enough. If you carry someone's heart, and she yours, then you *will* never part. But if you mean Princess Heart O'Stone, why that would be a very heavy burden indeed."

He saluted the fox, and they both sped away. Donnal went home thinking about the fox's words. But finally he laughed at himself, for when does a poor woodcutter get to carry a princess' heart?

The next day Donnal was outside, stacking wood into piles, when he heard a third cry for help, low and angry. It was not a plea but a demand. This time he found a bear in a pit.

Donnal puzzled for a moment, wondering if he should try to bring the bear up, when he noticed that it wore a collar with gold markings.

"That is no ordinary bear," said Donnal aloud. At the sound of his voice, the bear stood up and began twirling ever so slowly around and around in the pit.

Donnal lay down on his stomach, to look at the bear more

closely. It was the king's dancing bear, no doubt of it, though what it was doing so far from the castle, Donnal did not know.

"Just a minute, friend," he called. Then he leaped up and ran back home for his ax. He felled a nearby tree and with a chain dragged it to the pit, shoved it in partway, and the bear climbed out.

"And do you have thanks for me, too?" asked Donnal. He gave a small laugh then, for the bear stood on its hind legs and bowed. Then it ambled off without a word.

However, when the bear reached the edge of the clearing, it turned and looked back over it shoulder and growled:

> Heart of stone crack,
> Ride on your back.

Donnal thought about this. All three—the hawk, the fox, and the bear—had called out their thanks. Yet none of it had to do with Donnal and his rescuing. It all had to do with the princess. He remembered the stories about Princess Heart O'Stone, how she spent her time with birds and beasts and none at all with humans. He wondered if all the animals were her special friends. And then he called out to the bear. "Wait, wait for me," and ran after it, waving his hand.

The bear waited at the forest edge, and when Donnal caught up, it allowed the woodcutter to ride on its shoulders. They rode swifter than the winter wind and passed by the guards at the castle gate between one blink and the next. And when they came to the throne room, the bear pushed open the enormous door with its snout.

"What is this?" shouted the king to his flatterers and friends, and when none of them could answer, he asked the question of the bear.

At its master's voice, the bear bowed low, and Donnal slid over its head to the floor.

"I think I know how to help your daughter, Princess Heart O'Stone," said Donnal when he had picked himself up. "I may be only a poor woodcutter, but I can tell you what has been told me. It is here in my head."

"Then you shall part with it now," said the king in an angry yet controlled voice.

"The knowledge?" asked Donnal.

"No, woodcutter, your head," said the king. "For I have sworn to kill anyone who refers to the princess' problem."

"Wait," cried Donnal. "First listen and then take my head if you must. What I say will change your mind."

"I can change my mind no more than my poor daughter can change her heart," said the king.

The guards advanced on the woodcutter, their swords held high.

"It was the animals who told me," said Donnal.

"Wait," came a voice. And at that command, all motion in the throne room ceased for the voice belong to Princess Heart O'Stone herself and never before had she taken any interest in court proceedings.

She walked over to her father and stood by the throne. Her voice was low, but it could be heard throughout the room. "A handsome, brave lad riding in on a bear. If I *could* laugh, I would find that funny. Yet you want to behead him. If I *could*

cry, I would find that sad. But as I can do neither, at least I can listen. For I have found that people talk a lot and say nothing while animals talk infrequently and say much. A boy who has conversed with beasts is sure to say something interesting."

At her voice, Donnal looked up. And seeing her beauty, he looked down. He came over and knelt before her and spoke to the floor. It was all he could dare.

"Heart O'Stone is all alone," he whispered, for he knew at once it was true.

The princess reached down and held his chin in her hand, forcing him to look up at her. As Donnal looked into her eyes, he saw in those twin green pools his own fair reflection. And as he stared further, it seemed to him that in those pools was the faintest of ripples.

"I am," she said, *"all* alone. I thought no one had remarked it."

Then Donnal stood up and held both her hands in his.

At this, the king jumped up himself and would have cleaved Donnal's head from his shoulders with his own sword had not the queen put out a hand to stop him.

But Donnal did not notice. He saw only the princess. "I have remarked it," he said. "And it fairly breaks my heart to see you all alone. But you need not ever be alone again, for I am here."

"You?" said the princess.

And then Donnal added, *"Carry her heart, never part."*

The princess shook her head. "Would you dare carry such a burden?"

"If it were *your* heart, though truly made of stone, I would

68

carry it gladly," said Donnal. "And that would be a light task indeed for a back as straight and strong as mine."

Then the princess moved right up next to Donnal, and he spoke only to her. No one in the throne room but the princess heard his final words.

"Heart of stone crack, ride on my back," he said.

And as Donnal spoke, a great cracking sound was heard, as if the world itself were breaking in two. At that, the princess sighed. Tears ran down her cheeks and over her smiling mouth, but she never heeded them. She turned to her parents and cried out, "Mother, Father. I can laugh. I can cry. I can love."

She turned to Donnal, "And I will marry whom I will." She put her little hands on each side of his broad ones and brought them together as if in prayer.

"Marry him?" said the queen. "But he is a woodcutter. And besides, he is ill formed."

The courtiers all looked, and it was true. How could they have not seen it before. Donnal's face was beautiful still, but his proud straight back was now crooked. A hump, like a great stone, grew between his shoulders.

"She shall marry this man and no other," said the king, for while the others had been watching the princess all the time, he alone had kept his eyes on Donnal. He knew what it was that rested on the boy's shoulders. "He is a man of courage and compassion," said the king, "who knows the difference between advice and action. He shall carry the burdens of the kingdom on that crooked back with ease, of this I am sure."

So the two were married at once and ruled after the king

died. The princess was known for her laughter and her tears, which she was quick to give to any who asked. King Donnal Crookback never minded his hump, for the only mirrors he sought were the princess' eyes. And when they told him that he was straight and true, he knew they did not lie. And it was said, by all the people in the kingdom, that as loved as Queen Heart O'Stone was, King Donnal was more beloved still, for he had not one heart, but two: the one he carried hidden away in his breast, but the other he carried high between his shoulders, where it could be seen and touched by even the least of his people.

"*That's how I feel,*" *said the girl when the dream was done.* "*That I am carrying your heart, and it is no heavy burden.*"

But the boy directed his words to the Dream Weaver. "*The story was fine. Just meant for us.*"

"*Story?*" *the old woman said as she finished off the piece and held it out to him.* "*That was not just a story—but a woven dream. Here, take it. For your new life. Keep it safe.*"

The boy pushed her hand away gently. "*We do not need to take that with us, Dream Weaver. We have it safe—here.*" *He touched his hand to his chest.*

The girl, realizing the Dream Weaver could not see his gesture, added, "*Here in our hearts.*"

As if to make up for his tactlessness, and because he had a gentle nature, the boy said "Help us celebrate our good fortune, Dream Weaver." He dug into his pocket. "Here, I have one more coin. It is part of the marriage portion. We would have you weave yourself a tale."

The girl nodded, delighted with his words. "Yes, yes, please."

"Myself?" The old woman looked amazed. "All these years I have been on street corners, weaving dreams for a penny. Yet no one has ever suggested such a thing before. Weave for myself?"

"Were you never tempted to do one anyway?" It was the girl.

"Tempted?" The Dream Weaver put her head to one side, considering the question. "If I had been sighted, I might have been tempted. But the eye and ear are different listeners. So there was no need to weave a dream for myself. Besides . . . ," and she gave a short laugh. "Besides, it would have brought no coin."

They laughed with her. The boy took the Dream Weaver's hand and placed the coin gently in it, closing her fingers around the penny. "Here is the coin, then, for your own dream."

The Dream Weaver smiled a great smile that split her brown face in unequal halves. "You two watch closely for me, then. Be my eyes for the weaving. I shall hear the tale on my own."

And this was the tale that she wove.

❧ The Pot Child ☙

There was once an ill-humored potter who lived all alone and made his way by shaping clay into cups and bowls and urns. His pots were colored with the tones of the earth, and on their sides he painted all creatures excepting man.

"For there was never a human I liked well enough to share my house and my life with," said the bitter old man.

71

But one day, when the potter was known throughout the land for his sharp tongue as well as his pots, and so old that even death might have come as a friend, he sat down and on the side of a large bisque urn he drew a child.

The child was without flaw in the outline, and so the potter colored in its form with earth glazes: rutile for the body and cobalt blue for the eyes. And to the potter's practiced eye, the figure on the pot was perfect.

So he put the pot into the kiln, closed up the door with bricks, and set the flame.

Slowly the fires burned. And within the kiln the glazes matured and turned their proper tones.

It was a full day and a night before the firing was done. And a full day and a night before the kiln had cooled. And it was a full day and a night before the old potter dared unbrick the kiln door. For the pot child was his masterpiece, of this he was sure.

At last, though, he could put it off no longer. He took down the kiln door, reached in, and removed the urn.

Slowly he felt along the pot's side. It was smooth and still warm. He set the pot on the ground and walked around it, nodding his head as he went.

The child on the pot was so lifelike, it seemed to follow him with its lapis eyes. Its skin was a pearly yellow-white, and each hair on its head like beaten gold.

So the old potter squatted down before the urn, examining the figure closely, checking it for cracks and flaws, But there were none. He drew in his breath at the child's beauty and thought to himself. "*There* is one I might like well enough."

And when he expelled his breath again, he blew directly on the image's lips.

At that, the pot child sighed and stepped off the urn.

Well, this so startled the old man, that he fell back into the dust.

After a while, though, the potter saw that the pot child was waiting for him to speak. So he stood up and in a brusque tone said "Well, then, come here. Let me look at you."

The child ran over to him and, ignoring his tone, put its arms around his waist, and whispered "Father" in a high sweet voice.

This so startled the old man that he was speechless for the first time in his life. And as he could not find the words to tell the child to go, it stayed. Yet after a day, when he had found the words, the potter knew he could not utter them for the child's perfect face and figure had enchanted him.

When the potter worked or ate or slept, the child was by his side, speaking when spoken to but otherwise still. It was a pot child, after all, and not a real child. It did not join him in his work but was content to watch. When other people came to the old man's shop, the child stepped back onto the urn and did not move. Only the potter knew it was alive.

One day several famous people came to the potter's shop. He showed them all around, grudgingly, touching one pot and then another. He answered their questions in a voice that was crusty and hard. But they knew his reputation and did not answer back.

At last they came to the urn.

The old man stood before it and sighed. It was such an

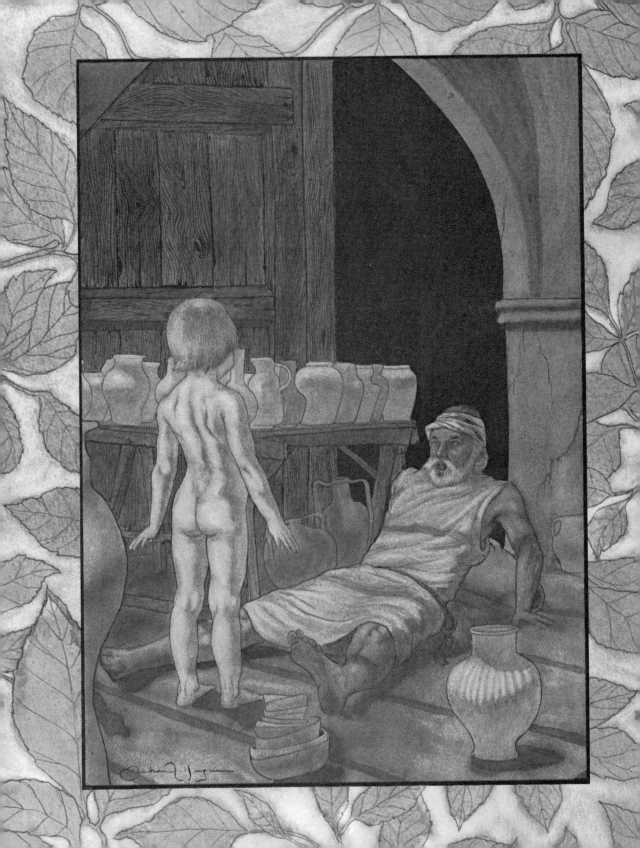

uncharacteristic sound that the people looked at him strangely. But the potter did not notice. He simply stood for a moment more, then said, "This is the Pot Child. It is my masterpiece. I shall never make another one so fine."

He moved away, and one woman said after him. "It *is* good." But turning to her companions, she added in a low voice, "But it is *too* perfect for me."

A man with her agreed. "It lacks something," he whispered back.

The woman thought a moment. "It has no heart," she said. "That is what is wrong."

"It has no soul," he amended.

They nodded at each other and turned away from the urn. The woman picked out several small bowls, and, paying for them, she and the others went away.

No sooner were the people out of sight than the pot child stepped down from the urn.

"Father," the pot child asked, "what is a heart?"

"A vastly overrated part of the body," said the old man gruffly. He turned to work the clay on his wheel.

"Then," thought the pot child, "I am better off without one." It watched as the clay grew first tall and then wide between the potter's knowing palms. It hesitated asking another question, but at last could bear it no longer.

"And what is a soul, Father?" asked the pot child. "Why did you not draw one on me when you made me on the urn?"

The potter looked up in surprise. "Draw one? No one can draw a soul."

The child's disappointment was so profound, the potter added, "A man's body is like a pot, which does not disclose what is inside. Only when the pot is poured, do we see its contents. Only when a man acts, do we know what kind of soul he has."

The pot child seemed happy with that explanation, and the potter went back to his work. But over the next few weeks the child continually got in his way. When the potter worked the clay, the pot child tried to bring him water to keep the clay moist. But it spilled the water and the potter pushed the child away.

When the potter carried the unfired pots to the kiln, the pot child tried to carry some, too. But it dropped the pots, and many were shattered. The potter started to cry out in anger, bit his tongue, and was still.

When the potter went to fire the kiln, the pot child tried to light the flame. Instead, it blew out the fire.

At last the potter cried, "You heartless thing. Leave me to do my work. It is all I have. How am I to keep body and soul together when I am so plagued by you?"

At these words, the pot child sat down in the dirt, covered its face, and wept. Its tiny body heaved so with its sobs that the potter feared it would break in two. His crusty old heart softened, and he went over to the pot child and said, "There, child. I did not mean to shout so. What it it that ails you?"

The pot child looked up. "Oh, my Father, I know I have no heart. But that is a vastly overrated part of the body. Still, I was trying to show how I was growing a soul."

The old man looked startled for a minute, but then,

recalling their conversation of many weeks before, he said "My poor pot child, no one can *grow* a soul. It is there from birth." He touched the child lightly on the head.

The potter had meant to console the child, but at that the child cried even harder than before. Drops sprang from its eyes and ran down its cheeks like blue glaze. "Then I shall never have a soul," the pot child cried. "For I was not born but made."

Seeing how the child suffered, the old man took a deep breath. And when he let it out again, he said, "Child, as I made you, now I will make you a promise. When I die, you shall have *my* soul for then I shall no longer need it."

"Oh, then I will be truly happy," said the pot child, slipping its little hand gratefully into the old man's. It did not see the look of pain that crossed the old man's face. But when it looked up at him and smiled, the old man could not help but smile back.

That very night, under the watchful eyes of the pot child, the potter wrote out his will. It was a simple paper, but it took a long time to compose for words did not come easily to the old man. Yet as he wrote, he felt surprisingly lightened. And the pot child smiled at him all the while. At last, after many scratchings out, it was done. The potter read the paper aloud to the pot child.

"It is good," said the pot child. "You do not suppose I will have long to wait for my soul?"

The old man laughed. "Not long, child."

And then the old man slept, tired after the late night's labor. But he had been so busy writing, he had forgotten to bank his fire, and in the darkest part of the night, the flames went out.

In the morning the shop was ice cold, and so was the old man. He did not waken, and without him, the pot child could not move from its shelf.

Later in the day, when the first customers arrived, they found the old man. And beneath his cold fingers lay a piece of paper that said:

> When I am dead, place my body in
> my kiln and light the flames. And
> when I am nothing but ashes, let
> those ashes be placed inside the
> Pot Child. For I would be one, body
> and soul, with the earth I have worked.

So it was done as the potter wished. And when the kiln was opened up, the people of the town placed the ashes in the ice-cold urn.

At the touch of the hot ashes, the pot cracked: once across the breast of the child and two small fissures under its eyes.

"What a shame," said the people to one another on seeing that. "We should have waited until the ashes cooled."

Yet the pot was still so beautiful, and the old potter so well known, that the urn was placed at once in a museum. Many people came to gaze on it.

One of those was the woman who had seen the pot that day so long ago at the shop.

"Why, look," she said to her companions. "It is the pot the old man called his masterpiece. It *is* good. But I like it even better now with those small cracks."

"Yes," said one of her companions, "it was too perfect before."

"Now the pot child has real character," said the woman. "It has . . . heart."

"Yes," added the same companion, "it has soul."

And they spoke so loudly that all the people around them heard. The story of their conversation was printed and repeated throughout the land, and everyone who went by the pot stopped and murmured, as if part of a ritual, "Look at that pot child. It has such heart. It has such soul."

"*Ah*," *sighed the Dream Weaver when the tale was done. It was a great relief to her to have it over, both the weaving and the telling. She dropped her hands to her sides and thought about the artist of the tale and how he alone really knew when his great work was done, and how he had put his own heart and soul into it. For what was art, she thought, but the heart and soul made visible.*

"*I thank you, my young friends,*" *she said to the boy and girl as they waited, hand upon hand, until she was through. "And now I can go home and sleep.*"

She finished the piece of weaving and held it up to them. "Will you take this one with you?" she asked.

"*But it was your dream,*" *said the boy hesitantly.*

The girl was more honest still. "There is nothing on it, Dream Weaver. On that — or on the other."

"Nothing? What do you mean—nothing?" Her voice trembled.

"A jumble of threads," said the girl. "Tightly woven, true, but with no picture or pattern."

"No picture? Nothing visible? Was there never a picture?" asked the old woman, her voice low.

"While you told the tale," said the boy, "there were pictures aplenty in my head and in my heart."

"And on the cloth?"

"I do not really know," admitted the girl. "For your voice spun the tale so well, I scarcely knew anything more."

"Ah," said the Dream Weaver. She was silent for a moment and then said, more to herself than to the two, "So that is why no one takes their dreams."

"We will take your weaving if it would please you," said the boy.

The Dream Weaver put away her loom and threads. "It does not matter," she said. "I see that now. Memory is the daughter of the ear and the eye. I know you will take the dream with you, in your memory, and it will last long past the weaving."

They helped her strap the baskets to her back. "Long past," they assured her. Then they watched as the Dream Weaver threaded her way down the crooked streets to her home.